W9-CPQ-032

Picture-Perfect TOMMY

Based on the TV series *Rugrats*® created by Arlene Klasky, Gabor Csupo, and Paul Germain as seen on Nickelodeon®

No part of this publication may be reproduced in whole or in part,
or stored in a retrieval system, or transmitted in any form or by any means,
electronic, mechanical, photocopying, recording, or otherwise,
without written permission of the publisher.
For information regarding permission, write to
Simon Spotlight, an imprint of Simon & Schuster Children's Publishing Division,
1230 Avenue of the Americas, New York, NY 10020.

ISBN 0-439-32288-X

Copyright © 2001 by Viacom International Inc.
All rights reserved.
NICKELODEON, *Rugrats*, and all related titles, logos,
and characters are trademarks of Viacom International Inc.
Published by Scholastic Inc., 555 Broadway, New York, NY 10012,
by arrangement with Simon Spotlight,
an imprint of Simon & Schuster Children's Publishing Division.
SCHOLASTIC and associated logos are trademarks and/or
registered trademarks of Scholastic Inc.

12 11 10 9 8 7 6 5 4 3 2 1   1 2 3 4 5 6/0

Printed in the U.S.A.

First Scholastic printing, September 2001

Picture-Perfect TOMMY

by Sarah Willson

illustrated by Robert Roper

SCHOLASTIC INC.

New York Toronto London Auckland Sydney
Mexico City New Delhi Hong Kong Buenos Aires

4

"The kids love to paint," said Didi.
"Let's go to the Fine Art Museum."
"Sounds great," Betty said.
"Aw, Deed," cried Stu.
"There's a great ball game on TV!"
Didi gave Stu a look.
Stu sighed. "Okay. I'll tell Chas
and Howard we're leaving."

Didi picked up Dil.
She put him into his stroller.
Dil picked up Tommy's painting.
He put it into his stroller.

At the museum, Stu looked at a painting. "You call this *fine* art?" he said. "Please. This looks like something Tommy would do."

"Oh, Stu," said Didi, shaking her head.

Dil pulled out Tommy's picture and dropped it on the floor.

NOSE
ART TEEST

9

"Look!" said Didi. "There's the gift shop!"

"Look!" said Stu. "There's the ball game!
You go ahead," he said to Didi and
Betty. "We'll watch the kids."

The fathers watched the game.
The babies crawled away.

A guard picked up Tommy's picture.

He looked at it.
He looked at the painting on the wall.
Then the guard hurried away.

"What is this place called, Tommy?" asked Chuckie.

"It's called the Find Art You-See-'Um," Tommy replied. "I think people find art here. And you-see-'um on the walls!"

BALLERINA
ITSA FLOP

SOGGY FIVE
WILD FRED

The babies crawled past the guard.
He was showing something
to another grown-up.

"It must have been hidden
behind a painting!" said the other man.
"We must put it up right away!"

"I like this one," said Tommy.
"I wonder if the baby who made it
got in trouble for cutting up the newspaper."

"Is he on the potty?" asked Chuckie.
"I think so," said Tommy.

19

"That baby must have used up a lot of markers doing all those dots," said Phil.

DOTS DA
BEACH
ED
STIRPOT

20

"This baby didn't even have to clean up his spilled paint," said Lil.

MESSY CANVAS
JACKIE PULLOCK

"That baby had trouble staying inside the lines," said Kimi.

CRACK
UP
KOOKIE

GIRL #601
ANDY HEEHAW

SELF PORTRAIT
MARK BOFFO

"This baby didn't know what to draw,"
said Chuckie.

"Look!" said Phil. "That baby got to draw on the wall!"

GOT SOUP?
G. WHIZZ

Just then Stu and Chas and Howard dashed around a corner.

"Weeee!" said Dil.

"There you are!" said Stu.

"We thought we'd lost you guys," said Chas.

"Let's go find your mom," Stu said to Tommy.

Dil pointed at a painting.
"Tomby!" he said excitedly.

"Hey, Tommy, isn't that your painting?"
Chuckie whispered.

"Yeah," said Tommy. "I guess they
finded my art. They must have wanted it
for the you-see-'um!"

"Look," said Didi, coming out of
the gift shop. "The kids like that painting!"
"I like it too," Stu said.
"But I still don't get this modern art.
Even Tommy could have done
a better job than some of these."

OOPS!
MEL DRIPPO

Stu chuckled. "Keep painting, sport. Maybe someday you'll have something hanging in here!"

ITLED
OODY

GREAT WORK
T HAS JUST
OUND. IT IS
ABLY FROM
TIST'S EARLY
SEE HOW THE
NT HAS BEEN
LY MIXED. RED
ELLOW HAVE
USED FOR
TIC EFFECT.

USEUM STAFF